To my first great-granddaughter, Zion McKenzie Noel
and to all things that squeal, purr, roar, hoot, screech,
bark, meow, chirp, and neigh. —J. P.

JERRY PINKNEY

THE LION & THE MOUSE

LITTLE, BROWN AND COMPANY
Books for Young Readers
New York   Boston

Putt-
Putt-
Putt

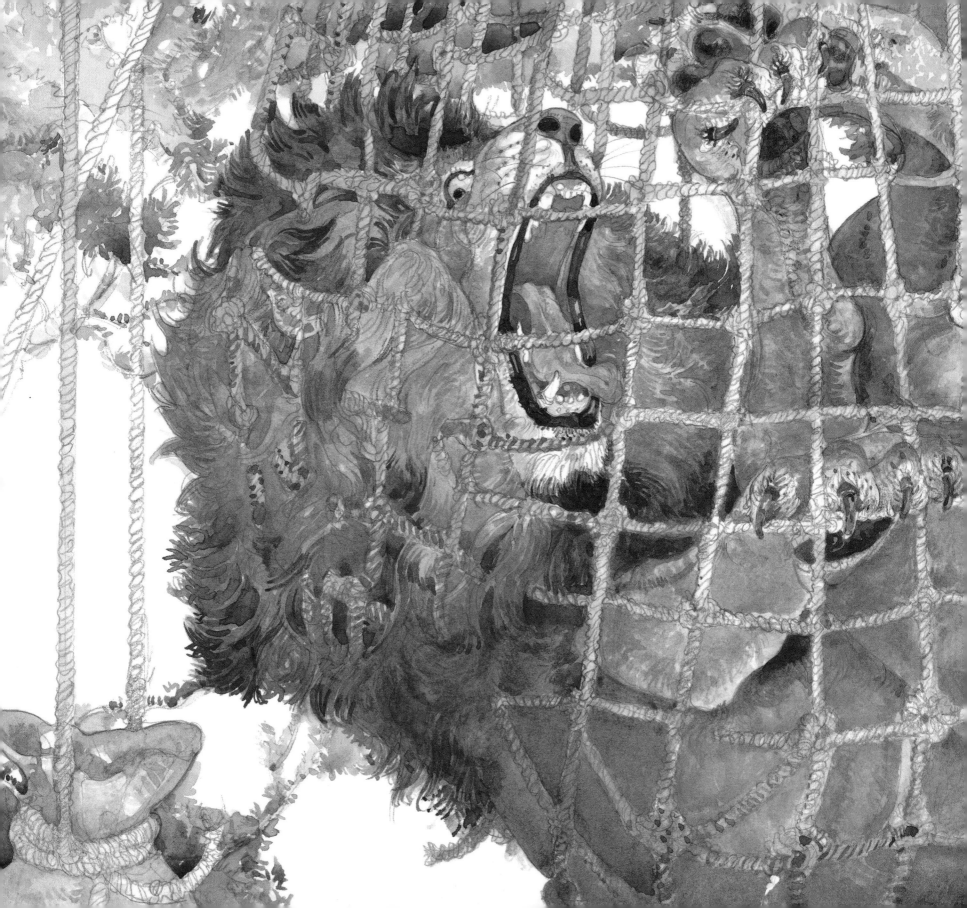

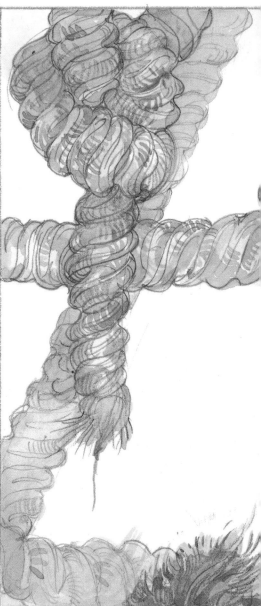

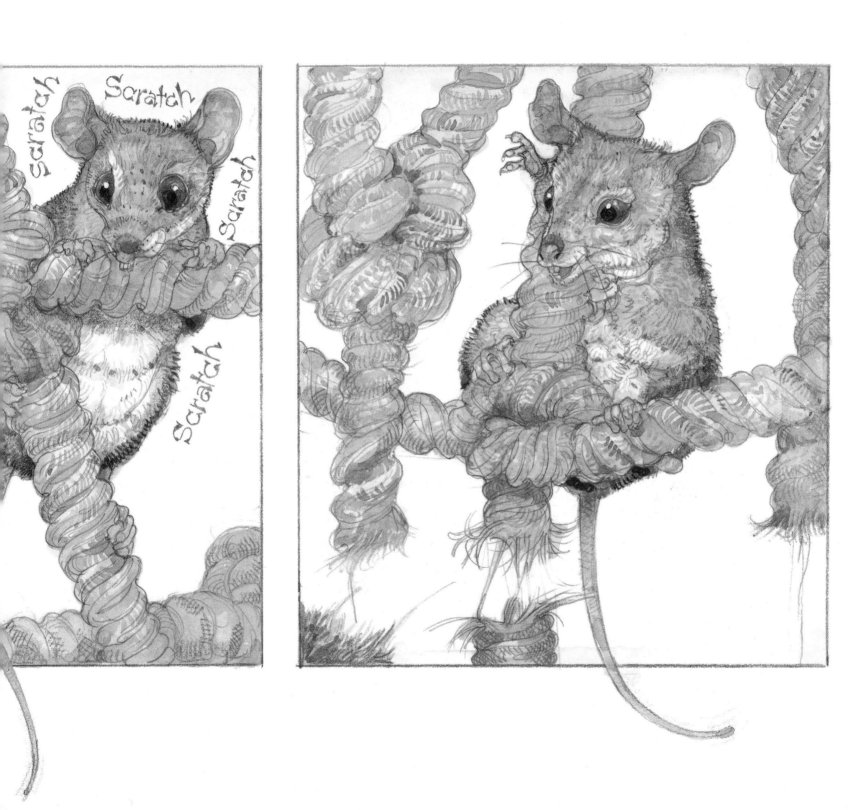

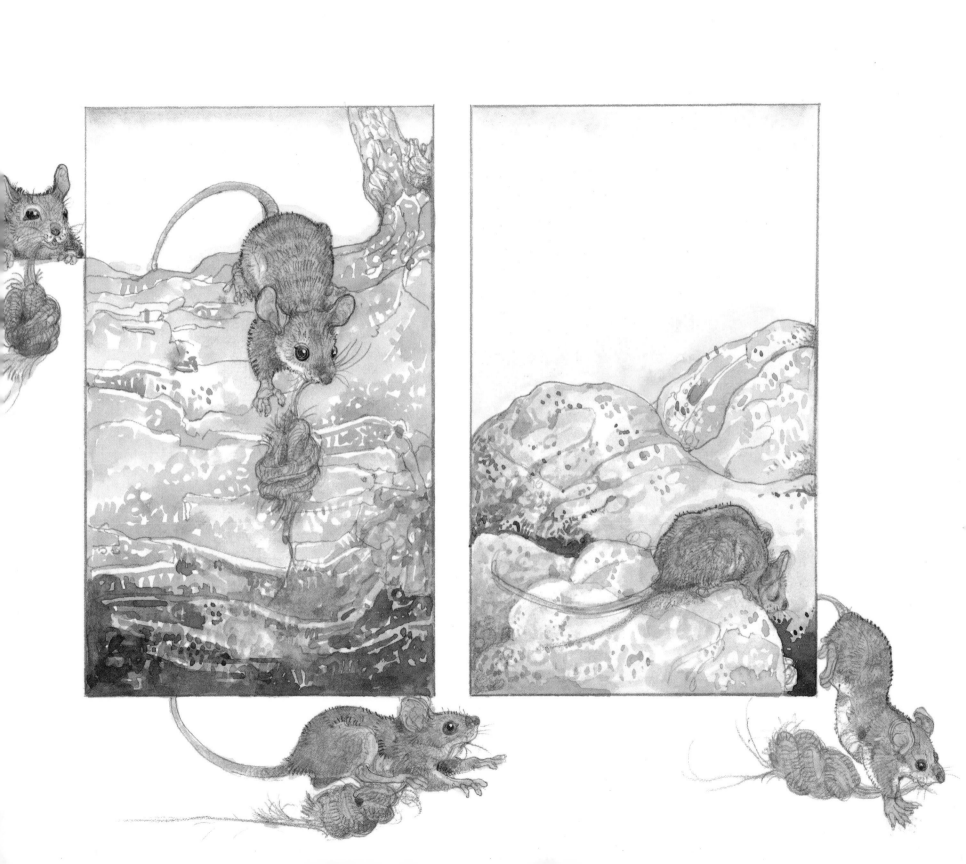

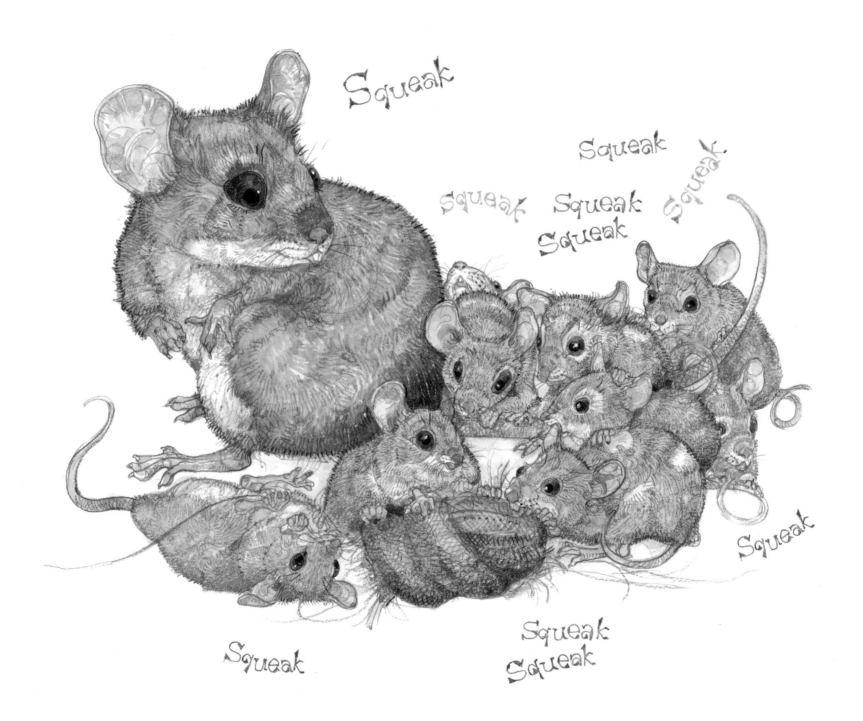

ARTIST'S NOTE

Of all Aesop's fables, "The Lion and the Mouse" is one of my childhood favorites: the tale of a mouse who accidentally disturbs a lion from his rest, and the lion who makes a life-changing decision to release his prey. When the mouse remembers her debt, she frees the lion from a poacher's trap. For me, this story offers far more than a simple moral of how the meek can trump the mighty.

Since working on my collection *Aesop's Fables*, I have felt drawn back to these two seemingly opposite characters. As a child I was inspired to see the majestic king of the jungle saved by the determination and hard work of a humble rodent; as an adult I've come to appreciate how both animals are *equally* large at heart: the courageous mouse, and the lion who must rise above his beastly nature to set his small prey free. It was gratifying, then, to place these two spirited creatures head-to-head on this book's jacket, each commanding powerful space and presence.

Since most retellings of the classic are sparse in text, a wordless version seemed quite natural; yet these engaging characters led me to make the story even fuller by providing a sense of family and setting. Living next to a nature preserve, I am fascinated with the vast medley of sounds coming from the surrounding woods, and that chorus of chatters and squeals helped shape the idea of selectively using animal sounds to gently enhance the story, while allowing the visuals—as well as the reader's imagination—to drive the narrative.

My curiosity and reverence for animal life has grown over the years, and my concern for them grows in equal measure. It seemed fitting, then, to stage this fable in the African Serengeti of Tanzania and Kenya, with its wide horizon and abundant wildlife so awesome yet fragile—not unlike the two sides of each of the heroes starring in this great tale for all times.

Jerry Pinkney